Dear Parents,

Welcome to the Scholastic Reader series. We have taken over 80 years of experience with teachers, parents, and children and put it into a program that is designed to match your child's interests and skills.

Level 1—Short sentences and stories made up of words kids can sound out using their phonics skills and words that are important to remember.

Level 2—Longer sentences and stories with words kids need to know and new "big" words that they will want to know.

Level 3—From sentences to paragraphs to longer stories, these books have large "chunks" of texts and are made up of a rich vocabulary.

Level 4—First chapter books with more words and fewer pictures.

It is important that children learn to read well enough to succeed in school and beyond. Here are ideas for reading this book with your child:

- Look at the book together. Encourage your child to read the title and make a prediction about the story.
- Read the book together. Encourage your child to sound out words when appropriate. When your child struggles, you can help by providing the word.
- Encourage your child to retell the story. This is a great way to check for comprehension.
- Have your child take the fluency test on the last page to check progress.

Scholastic Readers are designed to support your child's efforts to learn how to read at every age and every stage. Enjoy helping your child learn to read and love to read.

—**Francie Alexander**
Chief Education Officer
Scholastic Education

For the Gómez boys: Leonardo, Felipe,
Mateo, and Ruben
—R.G.

For my friend Terri
—M.M.

ISBN 0-439-44160-9

Text copyright © 2003 by Rebecca Gómez.
Illustrations copyright © 2003 by Mary Morgan.
Activities copyright © 2004 Scholastic Inc.
All rights reserved. Published by Scholastic Inc.
SCHOLASTIC, CARTWHEEL BOOKS, and associated logos
are trademarks and/or registered trademarks of Scholastic Inc.

18 17 16 15 14 13   08 09 10/0

Printed in the U.S.A. 23 • First trade edition printing, February 2004

It's
St. Patrick's Day!

by Rebecca Gómez
Illustrated by Mary Morgan

Scholastic Reader — Level 1

SCHOLASTIC INC.
New York Toronto London Auckland Sydney
Mexico City New Delhi Hong Kong Buenos Aires

It's St. Patrick's Day!
The holiday is here.

It's March 17th,
the same day every year.

It's St. Patrick's Day!

We love to dress in green.

Irish eyes will smile.

Will leprechauns be seen?

It's St. Patrick's Day!
Hurry up, get dressed.

There's a lot to celebrate.
You'll want to look your best.

It's St. Patrick's Day!
So wear a lot of green.

Choose hats, coats, shirts,
or anything in between!

It's St. Patrick's Day!
Let's find a four-leaf clover.

We'll celebrate the Irish
before the day is over.

It's St. Patrick's Day!
Let's make some Irish stew—

add potatoes, carrots, onions.
Serve it hot for me and you.

It's St. Patrick's Day!
We can dance an Irish reel.

We will drink sweet green juice
at each and every meal!

It's St. Patrick's Day!

Tune the harp and tune the fiddle.

We'll eat our favorite cookies,

with green icing in the middle!

It's St. Patrick's Day!
No matter where you were born,

today you can be Irish
and wish everyone "Top o' the morn!"

It's St. Patrick's Day!
Let's sing an Irish song.

We'll wear our green carnations
and celebrate all day long.

It's St. Patrick's Day!
Do you hear the pipes and drums?

Let's join the celebration.
Do you want to come?

It's St. Patrick's Day!
Irish music will be played.

Be sure to get to Main Street
to watch the big PARADE!

Happy St. Patrick's Day!